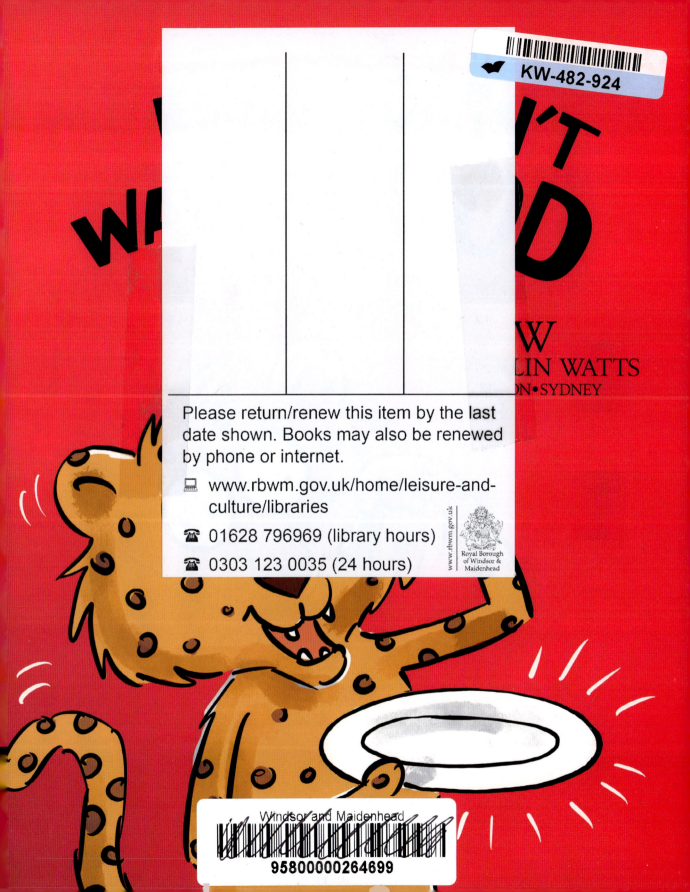

Leopard was always **wasting food**. At breakfast, he was often careless putting fruit into his bowl. Most of it went on the table and got squashed! He was careless pouring out his drink too.

4

His brother said he shouldn't waste food like that. He said he should be **more careful**. But Leopard took no notice!

Leopard always liked to make his own school lunch.
But he **didn't think** and made **silly choices**.
Once, he made green jelly sandwiches. They made
such a mess in his lunch box that he couldn't eat them.
He had to put them in the bin.

Monkey said he should think carefully about the food he made.

One day, Miss Bird had a surprise. She said they were going to visit a farm to find out how food was grown. Everyone was excited.

The farmer showed them everything he grew.

He said it was hard work to grow enough for everybody.

It **took lots of water** and **cost a lot of money**.

He said it was important not to waste food.

9

After school, everyone went to Wolf's party.

Mr Wolf had made lots of delicious things to eat.

He said everyone could help themselves.

But Leopard didn't think about how much he could eat.

He took so much that he **couldn't finish it all**!

Worst still, Leopard took the last sandwich and only took a few bites of it.

Monkey said he would have liked the sandwich and he would have **eaten it all up** and not wasted it. Everyone was cross with Leopard.

Leopard was upset. He didn't like everyone being cross with him. He was sorry for wasting food. He went to talk to Mum.

He told her about the farm visit. He told her about Wolf's party. He said he wished he **didn't waste food**.

Mum listened carefully. She said there were lots of things Leopard could do to stop wasting food. She said she always made a meal plan. Then she knew **how much food** to buy or what to pick from the garden.

16

She said she **stored food carefully** so that it didn't go stale. Leopard said he could do that.

The next morning, Leopard put the fruit in his bowl carefully. He poured out his drink carefully, too. He put all the food he didn't need back in the fridge to keep it cool and fresh.

His brother said he was pleased Leopard **hadn't wasted food**.

19

Then Leopard made a **lunch plan** for the week.
He thought carefully about what he'd like to eat
and wrote it all down in his best writing.
Then he made some delicious sandwiches.
He made **just the right amount**. He wrapped
them carefully in paper to keep them fresh.

Then he picked some fruit from the garden. He put it carefully in his lunch box. Mum was pleased.

At lunchtime, Leopard **ate all his sandwiches**.

Miss Bird said she was pleased he hadn't wasted any.

But just then, the bell went for the end of lunch break. Leopard didn't have time to eat his fruit. He didn't want to waste it. Then he had a good idea.

After school, Leopard took the fruit home. He asked Dad to help him make a smoothie with it. Dad said that was a **clever way** to use up leftover fruit.

Soon the smoothie was ready. It smelled delicious. It tasted delicious. Everyone said it was **the best smoothie ever**.

Leopard felt proud. He said it was important **not to waste food**. He said it was important to **use it all up**. He said it was important to eat it all up, too.

Everyone agreed!

A note about sharing this book

The *Nature Matters* series has been developed to provide a starting point for further discussion on how children might learn ways in which they could help the environment. It provides opportunities to explore ways of developing children's understanding of the importance of caring for nature and how, both as individuals and as a community, we can all contribute towards safeguarding the environment.

The series is set in the jungle with animal characters reflecting typical levels of understanding about nature and the world around us, often seen in young children.

Leopard Doesn't Waste Food

This story looks at how children might learn about the importance of not wasting food in order to help the environment. It also suggests, in simple terms, how to use up leftover food and how to store food sensibly and safely.

How to use the book

The book is designed for adults to share with either an individual child, or a group of children, and as a starting point for discussion. The book also provides visual support and repeated words and phrases to build reading confidence.

Before reading the story

Choose a time to read when you and the children are relaxed and have time to share the story.

Spend time looking at the illustrations and talk about what the book might be about before reading it together.

Encourage children to employ a phonics-first approach to tackling new words by sounding the words out.

After reading, talk about the book with the children:

- Talk about how Leopard wasted food. Can the children recall all the things he did? Do the children perhaps have younger brothers or sisters who are not as careful as they are when pouring out drinks or putting food on a plate or into a bowl? Invite them to share their observations.

- Why do they think it is important only to take the right amount of food? Why is it wasteful to take more than you can eat?

- Why was it a good idea for Leopard's mum to make a meal plan? How does that stop food wastage?

- Talk about using leftover food. Do the children have any favourite meals at home where leftovers are used? Examples might be soups from leftover vegetables, stir fries and smoothies.

Remind the children to listen carefully while others speak and to wait for their turn.

- Provide the children with a plain sheet of paper. Ask them to draw a plate of food that they would like for lunch. Ask them to draw the amount they could eat without wasting any. For example; two fish fingers, a spoonful of vegetables, a spoonful of potatoes.

- Point out that everyone has different-sized appetites. However, the important thing is to take only what you can eat up without wasting any.

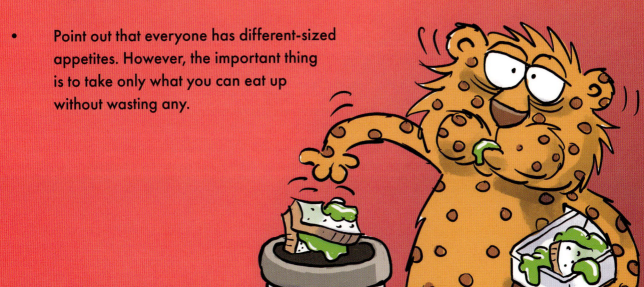

For Isabelle, William A, William G, George, Max, Emily,
Leo, Caspar, Felix, Tabitha, Phoebe, Harry and Libby –S.G.

Franklin Watts
First published in 2025 by
Hodder and Stoughton

Text © Hodder and Stoughton Ltd, 2025
Illustrations © Trevor Dunton 2025

The right of Trevor Dunton to be identified as the illustrator
of this Work has been asserted in accordance with the
Copyright, Designs and Patents Act, 1988.

Editor: Jackie Hamley
Designers: Cathryn Gilbert and Peter Scoulding

A CIP catalogue record for this book is available
from the British Library.

ISBN 978 1 4451 8677 1 (hardback)
ISBN 978 1 4451 8676 4 (paperback)
ISBN 978 1 4451 9267 3 (ebook)

Printed in China

Franklin Watts
An imprint of
Hachette Children's Books,
Part of Hodder and Stoughton
Carmelite House
50 Victoria Embankment
London EC4Y 0DZ

An Hachette UK company
www.hachettechildrens.co.uk

The authorised representative in the EEA is Hachette Ireland, 8 Castlecourt Centre,
Castleknock Road, Castleknock, Dublin 15, D15 YF6A, Ireland

MIX
Paper | Supporting
responsible forestry
FSC® C104740
FSC
www.fsc.org